We hope you enjoy this book.
Please return or renew it by the due date.
You can renew it at **www.norfolk.gov.uk/libraries**
or by using our free library app. Otherwise you can
phone **0344 800 8020** - please have your library
card and pin ready.
You can sign up for email reminders too.

NORFOLK COUNTY COUNCIL
LIBRARY AND INFORMATION SERVICE

NORFOLK ITEM

3 0129 08826 8249

D1494724

NO' ... BLU ... OU, ... O!

Emma Chichester Clark

HarperCollins *Children's Books*

For April, daughter of Lily Brown

First published in the United Kingdom by HarperCollins *Children's Books* in 2023
HarperCollins *Children's Books* is a division of HarperCollins*Publishers* Ltd
1 London Bridge Street
London SE1 9GF

www.harpercollins.co.uk

HarperCollins*Publishers*
Macken House, 39/40 Mayor Street Upper
Dublin 1, D01 C9W8, Ireland

10 9 8 7 6 5 4 3 2 1

Text and illustrations copyright © Emma Chichester Clark 2023

ISBN: 978-0-00-849191-8

Emma Chichester Clark asserts the moral right to be identified as the author and illustrator of the work. A CIP catalogue record for this title is available from the British Library. All rights reserved. This book is sold subject to the condition that it shall not, by way of trade or otherwise, be lent, re-sold, hired out or otherwise circulated without the publisher's prior consent in any form, binding or cover other than that in which it is published and without a similar condition including this condition being imposed on the subsequent purchaser. No part of this publication may be reproduced, stored in a retrieval system or transmitted in any form or by any means, electronic, mechanical, photocopying, recording or otherwise, without the prior permission of HarperCollins*Publishers* Ltd.

Printed in the UK

Blue Kangaroo belonged to Lily.
He was her very own kangaroo. They went everywhere together. Lily always said, "I'm not going anywhere without you, Blue Kangaroo!"

They went to
school together.

They went shopping
together.

They went to the park together.

When Lily's mother asked,
"Are you coming, Lily?"
Lily would say, "Not without
you, Blue Kangaroo!"

It had always been like that, ever since Blue Kangaroo
first arrived.

And Blue Kangaroo
hoped it always would be.

One day, Lily's friends Lulu and Poppy came over.
They all ran upstairs to play dressing-up in Lily's room.

"Oh! Look, Poppy!" said Lulu, laughing. "Lily still has her Blue Kangaroo. We don't have cuddly toys any more, Lily!" she said.

"Really?" asked Lily.
"No, we're too old for them now," said Lulu.
"Yes," said Poppy. "You'll have to give Blue Kangaroo to your little brother."

Just then, Lily's little brother, Jack, marched in. He picked up Blue Kangaroo and marched out again. Lily said nothing.

Oh no! thought Blue Kangaroo. *Surely, she won't give me to the baby . . .*

The next day, Aunt Jemima said, "Let's go to the museum!"
Lily put Blue Kangaroo in her special bag and said,
"I'm not going without you, Blue Kangaroo!"

The first thing they saw was a Dodo. Aunt Jemima said it
was "extinct".
"Ex-stink!" cried Jack. "Stinky stink!"
Then Lily noticed some older boys from her school.

The boys were following behind them, looking at the
stuffed animals. But Lily thought they were looking at her.

They were whispering and pointing and giggling.
Were they laughing at her because she had a cuddly toy?

Lily quickly shoved Blue
Kangaroo into her little
brother's arms.

Oh, Lily, thought Blue
Kangaroo. *Why do you care
what they think?*

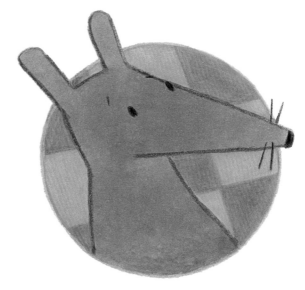

On the way home, Lily tried to get Blue Kangaroo back,
but Jack wouldn't let go. Then, suddenly, a huge great
hairy dog raced towards them.

It snatched Blue Kangaroo and galloped away.

"Nooooo!" cried Lily. "Come back! That's my kangaroo!"

She ran as fast as she could.

Luckily, the park keeper stopped the huge great hairy dog and told him to *sit*. Then he gently prised Blue Kangaroo from its mouth.

The park keeper gave Blue Kangaroo
to Jack and everyone clapped.

"Mine!" said Jack.

Lily said nothing, and Blue
Kangaroo felt very disappointed
about that.

Later on, Lulu's mother rang and asked if Lily would
like to go for a sleepover at their house.
"Can I?" asked Lily.
"Yes, I think you're old enough now," said her mother.

Lily was very excited.
"But I'll have to go without you,
Blue Kangaroo," she said.

Oh, no! thought Blue Kangaroo.
I always go everywhere with you . . .

That night, Lily fell asleep and Blue Kangaroo lay
awake worrying.
A whole night without Lily . . . thought Blue
Kangaroo – and he knew Lily would miss him too.

Then he had a brilliant idea . . .

In the morning, Lily searched all over the house for
Blue Kangaroo.
"I'm afraid that naughty Jack must have taken him to
Aunt Florence's house," said Lily's mother.

She packed pyjamas and a toothbrush in Lily's rucksack for the sleepover.

"I've never spent a night without Blue Kangaroo," said Lily.

"He'll be here when you get back," said her mother.

At Lulu's house, Lily and Lulu and Poppy had pizzas, but Lily didn't feel very hungry.

Then they played the Wacky Dance Dice Roll game, but Lily's heart wasn't really in it.

And then Lulu showed
Lily where she was
going to sleep, and
Lily thought of her
own bed with Blue
Kangaroo in it.

*How will I ever get to sleep
without Blue Kangaroo?*
she wondered.

She pulled her pyjamas
out of her rucksack . . .
and guess what she found!

"Blue Kangaroo!" cried Lily. "How did you get here?"
"Lily!" said Poppy. "You know we're too old for cuddly toys!"

"Well, maybe I'm not!" said Lily.

And Blue Kangaroo's heart swelled with pride.

"Well . . ." said Lulu.
"Actually, in fact . . .
I'm not either."
And she pulled a brown,
furry teddy out from
under her pillow.

"Oh!" said Poppy.
"Well, then I'd better
get Petronella out!"
And out came a very
squashed, floppy, pink
rabbit.

After they'd introduced the bear and the rabbit and Blue
Kangaroo to each other, all the fun began.

They played games and ate all kinds of not-very-grown-up things, and it was perfect.

Before she went to sleep that night, Lily said,
"I'm never, ever going anywhere, ever again, without you,
Blue Kangaroo!"

And Blue Kangaroo fell asleep in her arms.